The Easter Sparrows

Written by Michael J. Larson

Illustrations by Janine Ringdahl Schmidt

WestBow Press
A Division of Thomas Nelson & Zondervan
1663 Liberty Drive
Bloomington, IN 47403
www.westbowpress.com
844-714-3454

ISBN: 978-1-4497-0012-6 (sc)
ISBN: 978-1-4497-5084-8 (e)

Library of Congress Control Number: 2009942971

Print information available on the last page.

WestBow Press rev. date: 04/21/2022

WESTBOW
PRESS®
A DIVISION OF THOMAS NELSON
& ZONDERVAN

The author would like to dedicate this book
to his wife Kathie
and her friend Shirley.

The illustrator would like to dedicate this book
to her husband Alan
and their three wonderful children,
Hannah, Nora, and Nelson, for all
the encouragement they have given her.

Chip and Chirp were perched on a rock ledge. The two sparrows fluffed their feathers to keep out the evening cold.

"Are you sure this is a safe place to spend the night?" asked Chip.

"I'm sure," replied Chirp. "No one's going to come into a tomb in the middle of the night."

"W-W-We're roosting in a tomb?" questioned Chip. "That's for dead people isn't it?'

"Yes," Chirp answered. "But this is a new tomb and it has never been used. Joseph, a rich man from Arimathea, had it built. He is healthy and he won't need it for a long time."

"Oh, that's good news!"exclaimed Chip.

The two birds snuggled together on the rocky ledge and were soon fast asleep.

Suddenly the dark of the tomb gave way to the flicker of torchlight. Chip and Chirp awoke with a start and watched fearfully as the tomb filled with people.

Joseph, the rich man who owned the tomb, said, "I had this tomb cut out of rock for myself, but now we need to bury Jesus, the Son of God."

Many in the group were crying softly as Joseph continued, "I pray this tomb will be a worthy resting place for Jesus."

Chirp whispered, "They nailed Jesus, the Son of God, to a cross today. He died hanging on the cross."

"Why would the humans kill him?" asked Chip.

"They didn't believe he was the Son of God," replied Chirp.

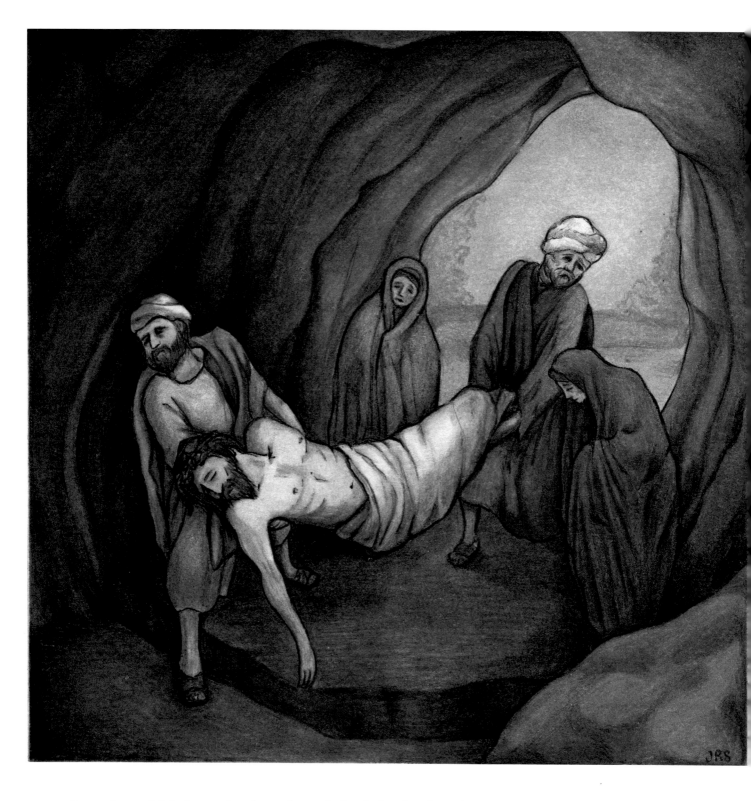

Joseph and his heartbroken friends laid the body of Jesus on the cold tomb floor.

They wrapped the body of Jesus from head to toe in strips of linen cloth. The tomb became dark again as the small group left.

Suddenly there was a loud scraping noise. It was the sound of rock meeting rock.

"They have rolled a stone over the tomb opening!" gasped Chip. "We're trapped in the tomb with the body of Jesus!"

They feared they would never see the light of day again.

Both birds were sleeping when a bright light filled the tomb.

"Wake up, Chirp!" gasped Chip. "Look, it is brighter than day, but the stone has not been rolled back."

Squinting, the surprised Chirp asked, "Where is the light coming from?"

The light seemed to have no source. It filled the tomb, and even the deepest cracks in the tomb walls were bathed in light.

"Look," gasped Chirp, "Jesus is sitting up and removing the linen strips. He is alive!"

"He has risen from the dead!" exclaimed Chip.

For several minutes the sparrows watched in shocked silence.

"Who are those two men helping him?" questioned Chip. "And how did they get in here?"

"I would guess those are angels sent from God to help Jesus," cried Chirp. "A sealed tomb could not keep angels out."

"Awesome!" cried the two sparrows.

"And the light is from God's presence," whispered Chip. "That's why it is so bright it fills even the darkest corners."

Jesus stood and the two birds saw his face for the first time. It was a face filled with peace, joy, and love.

Looking up at the roosting sparrows, Jesus said, "Are not two sparrows sold for a small coin? Yet not one of them falls to the ground without your Father's knowledge." (Matthew 10:29)

As Jesus finished talking, he and the two angels disappeared.

"Where did they go?" screamed Chirp.

"The rock is still blocking the tomb opening," added Chip. "How did they get out?"

Then Chirp spoke. "He said he was going to do this. Jesus said he would die and on the third day rise and we saw him do just that.

"He died for the sins of all humans. And now if people live their lives for Jesus when they die, they will live with him forever in Heaven," the sparrow continued.

"Wow," gasped Chip. "Think about that—living forever with God!"

Suddenly Chip shouted, "But now we are trapped in the tomb!"

"Now, Chip," soothed Chirp, "Jesus just told us his Father knows everything about us. He even knows if we fall to the ground."

"Then he must know we are trapped in the tomb," cried Chip. "He will save us!"

"We must have faith," added Chirp.

Suddenly the ground trembled and bits of rock clattered to the tomb floor.

"An earthquake!" shouted Chip

The rock blocking the tomb shuddered and slowly rolled away from the opening.

"The door is open!" cheered the sparrows as they flew and landed in the doorway.

Chip asked, "Did that earthquake cause the stone to roll away?"

"No," Chirp replied, "The angel moved it."

At that moment several women approached the tomb and the angel spoke to them, saying, "Do not be afraid! I know you are seeking Jesus, the crucified. He is not here, for he has been raised, just as he said. Come and see the place where he lay." (Matthew 28:5-6)

The two sparrows flew and landed on some nearby branches. Here they spent the day thinking about all they had just seen.

Finally, toward evening, Chirp said, "I wonder how many humans really understand what happened today."

"Those who understand will live changed lives," said Chip.

"That's for sure!"

At last, Chirp spread his wings. He said, "It's almost dusk and we need to find a new place to roost for the night."

"That's right, Chirp, but this time let's find a place that has doors and windows that can't be closed!"

So off Chirp and Chip flew.

Their stay in the tomb had changed them forever.

Will you, too, be changed by what they saw?

Author's Biography

For thirty-four years Michael J. Larson taught high school biology. He especially enjoyed teaching about the environment, so it is not surprising that his stories are told through the experiences of creatures found in nature.

His previous book, *Nature's Christmas Story*, involved tundra animals responding to the birth of the Christ Child.

Mr. Larson first wrote for children when he produced an environmental column for the magazine *Minnesota Out of Doors*, St. Paul, Minnesota. He later published the seventy-two columns resulting from the six-year writing stint in a three volume collection titled, *Children in the Outdoors*.

Although he is retired from full-time teaching he continues to develop environmental learning experiences for children as the director of the Bonanza Education Center along Big Stone Lake near Beardsley, Minnesota.

The author lives with his wife Kathie on a small acreage near the town of Wheaton, Minnesota. They have three grown children who have blessed the family with seven grandchildren.